Hysteria 2

Ten Winning Stories from the Hysteria 2013 Short Story Writing Competition

run by

The Hysterectomy Association.

Edited by Linda Parkinson-Hardman

Hysteria 2

Published by: The Hysterectomy Association

ISBN: 978-0-9927429-0-4

A catalogue record for this book is available from The British Library.

Telephone: 0843 289 2142

Website: www.hysterectomy-association.org.uk

CONTENTS

About the Hysteria Writing Competition

Hysteria is an annual writing competition for women only; it opens on the 1st April each year and closes at midnight on the 31st August. You can find out more on the Hysterectomy Association website about the next competition at:

hysterectomy-association.org.uk/hysteria-writing-competition/

Acknowledgements

The competition and this anthology wouldn't have been possible without the support and help of all the following people.

This book is dedicated to them and to the users of the Hysterectomy Association.

Thank you.
Linda Parkinson-Hardman (editor).

Judges

Ruby Cowling, Sophie Duffy, Rebecca Forste, Penelope Laurence, Anne Wilson

You can find out more about all our judges here:

hysterectomy-association.org.uk/hysteria-writing-competition/

Foreword

In 2012 we launched the Hysteria Writing Competition for the first time. We had no knowledge of whether it would be accepted by the writing community, neither if anyone would enter nor indeed if we would eventually publish our first anthology of winning entries.

I am pleased to say that it worked beautifully and our first anthology, Hysteria was published at the beginning of this year.

So we decided to do it again; this time with the plan that it would become an annual event.

Once again I was privileged to receive all the entries first; once again I was stunned and awed by the quality of the entries and was pleased I was not in the unenviable position of having to judge them.

I was also pleasantly surprised when some of last years winners came forward to act as judges and also when a runner up from Hysteria 1 was the overall winner in this year's competition. Now I'm looking forward to the competition for 2014, anticipating another exceptional journey through some wonderful reading material.

The following stories, there were no poems this year, cover another broad spectrum of female experience; children, aging, relationships and family - each are explored in some intriguing, entertaining and often thought provoking ways. Once again I commend them and once again I hope you enjoy them as much as the judges and I did.

Linda Parkinson-Hardman (Editor)

School is for Boys by Veronica Bright

Before it happened, the girl was happy.

On a typical school day, her shoes were waiting for her, by the door. Sturdy and strong. Soon after sunrise she would be wearing her flip-flops, which sent satisfying little puffs of dust up as she climbed the hill, her body bent. Soon she would be on the bus, as it growled its way along the narrow roads of Nepal. The girl imagined being a doctor, looking after people in one of the hospitals in Kathmandu. Her ambitions made her smile.

When the load on her head slipped, it dug into her flesh, and she bent further to ease the pressure. Up the hill, round the corner. One foot after another.

The week before it happened, she was excited. Some visitors were coming to school. The children would sing in Nepalese and English. Then they would talk with the foreigners.

"What is your name?" a visitor would say.

"My name is Rashmina," she'd reply. "I am ten years old."

Her teacher said she was a good worker, quick to learn. Last week she wrote about elephants, illustrating her page with an image she copied from a book. The teacher put it on the wall. Rashmina had never seen an elephant herself, but she knew a lot about monkeys. Sometimes they came swinging through the trees near her house, and she and her mother had to shout at them and throw stones to drive them away. Bold furry little things, they loved to eat the juicy oranges that hung from the branches.

Back at the house, Rashmina heaved her bundle to the ground. The goats pulled on their tethers in the shelter and bleated. When

Rashmina gave them the leafy branches, they munched quickly, their faces expressionless.

"One more load," her mother called. "We have plenty of time. The morning tea will be ready when you get back."

A grey cloud surged out of the door, threatening the yard. Her mother's eyes would be stinging, her nose full of smoke. Every sunrise was the same. Over and over again, the smoke had to learn that it is meant to go straight up, and out through the roof vent.

From somewhere in the valley, Rashmina could hear the put-put of an engine: her father's tractor, an ancient vehicle pulling a battered cart. Yet how proud his smile when he fetched it from Pokhara a month ago; when he drove it down to the hayfield, his whole family bumping up and down in the trailer, Rashmina, her younger brother Jhalak, and their mother. And what joy, what freedom Rashmina felt, walking home at the end of the day, with the sun on her back instead of a huge bundle of scratchy hay.

"Do not forget how hard I have worked for this tractor," her father had said. "I am the only one in the village to own such a fine piece of machinery. Even my brother down in the valley has not acquired a fine help-mate like this."

Rashmina patted one of the goats, and set off again, up to the road and back towards the fields where the hedges grew high, down the dusty curvy track. After the second bend she had a view of the river where the black kites circled.

An aeroplane droned overhead, and Rashmina looked up, imagining tourists, peering from windows, ready with their cameras and binoculars. Skybirds, Jhalak called them. Rashmina cut branches from the hedge, wielding the blade carefully. She lifted the load to her head.

When she arrived home, the milk tea was ready; the rice porridge bubbled in the pot on the fire; the smoke rose obediently. Rashmina ate, then went to the communal washing place, where the water was bracingly cold. Rashmina put on her uniform; her mother combed her hair, tied red ribbons at the ends of her plaits.

Lastly Rashmina put on the heavy black shoes and took her brother's hand. She was smiling as her mother kissed the children goodbye.

Rice wine. The Saturday before it happened, Rashmina spread out a stiff cloth in the yard, fetched a container full of grain, and poured it onto the fabric. Then she spread the grain with the palm of her hand as her mother had taught her. Her brother Jhalak watched. He was a listless boy, content to sit. Rashmina knew her mother worried about him. Her father said he would grow strong when he had to work on the farm.

Rashmina had seen her father after he had drunk too much rice wine. His feet wandered all over the place; his speech became slurred. Her mother said it was nothing to be concerned about. Men liked to drink rice wine, and it fortified them against the cold when they had to work into the night.

As Rashmina smoothed the grain, she talked to her brother. "Next week at school, when the visitors come, I'm going to practise my English." Her hand moved swiftly over the seeds. "When I take my exams they'll be in English."

Jhalak said nothing, but he smiled.

When Rashmina had finished spreading the rice, she put a dish of chillies out in the yard to dry, then she tied some maize together and hung it in bunches on the wall. She sat near the doorway with her little brother, and sang the songs they had learnt at school. Jhalak smiled but he didn't join in.

Their father came home for a meal. He stood in the yard overlooking his potato patch. Voices approached from the rugged path. It was one of the guides from the lodge with a group of walkers. Rashmina's father knew the guide well. They greeted each other, passed the time of day. Rashmina's father invited them to take a short cut through his property. The guide spoke in English to Rashmina.

"How are you today?"

"I am well thank you."

"This young lady is learning English," he announced. One of the foreigners smiled at Rashmina and asked, "What is your name?"

"My name is Rashmina. What is your name?"

The father looked on, proud of his daughter. He offered the foreigners oranges from his tree. They peeled them, taking the green and orange skins off. They exclaimed at the juiciness, the flavour.

They walked past the school uniforms drying on the bushes. Then they were gone.

After the sun had set for the day, Rashmina lay in bed and imagined the coming Monday, being on the school bus, looking out of the window as the children travelled along narrow roads, round winding bends, listening to the two-tone tune that warned other drivers that their bus was overtaking. All the English she had learnt sang softly in her mind. It seemed as if she had been waiting forever for this day.

Rashmina heard Jhalak breathing in the darkness, and she too fell asleep.

And before the next school day, it happens.

There are unfamiliar sounds, men shouting, a wail from her mother. Rashmina sits up quickly, slides out of bed. Jhalak creeps over to take her hand. She leads the way, pulling him gently. She calls for her mother. There is no-one in the house, no-one in the yard. Jhalak begins to whimper.

Outside there is nothing to see but dark shadows, and above the trees, stars. There is nothing to hear but the distant shouts of anxious men.

The children stand hand in hand, shivering.

The sun is waiting to creep over the Annapurnas when their mother returns. One of the neighbouring women is with her, propelling her in the right direction. Rashmina takes a step backwards, her mouth opening. Jhalak runs towards his mother. The neighbour speaks, words jerking out.

"Your father. An accident. His tractor. Down that slope. In the dark. So much work to do. Trying to get an early start. Rashmina, make up the fire, your mother needs tea."

"Rice wine." Rashmina's mother is weeping. "It was just a little. To warm him."

"The fire, Rashmina."

"Your father is dead."

Days pass. Rashmina's mother explains that they cannot keep the farm going without her father. Her uncle will come and fetch the tractor and trailer, and Rashmina and the hens will go back with him.

"Don't be afraid," says her mother. "There is a school in the valley. Your cousins both go there, and if you work hard for your uncle, he will let you go to school too."

Rashmina's mother will return to her own parents' house, and Jhalak and the goats will go with her.

The days are filled with work, with fetching water, cooking meals, washing clothes. But above all, they are filled with waiting. The mother and the girl weep often, with grief, with fatigue. The boy is silent; he seems smaller than ever. He never smiles.

In a moment of rest, Rashmina sits in the yard, her arm around the small bewildered Jhalak.

"When I am a doctor, I will have a house that you and our mother can live in.

"Where will it be?" His voice is tiny.

"In Kathmandu, perhaps, or Pokhara."

"I wish Father could come with us."

"He cannot come with us, Jhalak. He cannot come back."

Rashmina holds the small boy, and her mother comes and puts her arms around them both.

"Be a good girl, and work hard at your uncle's farm," she says.

"I will, I will."

When the uncle arrives, Rashmina's mother prepares a meal for him, treats him with great respect.

"This is good," he says. "I hope Rashmina will grow up to be a good cook."

The tractor and trailer are ready to go. Rashmina sits beside a basket of oranges. The hens are in a wicker cage. The girl hugs her mother and her brother. Weeping, Rashmina climbs up into the trailer.

The uncle speaks to her mother. "I will look after your daughter."

He starts the tractor. It lets out a cloud of dark smoky exhaust, and they're off. Rashmina turns and looks back at her mother and brother until her uncle drives round the bend, and she cannot see them any more.

At the uncle's house she is greeted fondly by her aunt. The cousins point to the pallet where she will sleep. The aunt shows her where to put her clothes. Rashmina unwraps her bundle. She takes her school shoes out and smiles.

"Well, well, well," says the uncle.

"Oh dear," says the aunt.

"I will work for you," Rashmina says, "before and after school. I will do all I can to help. I am a good worker."

Her uncle stands up. His silence alarms her. She feels a lump in her throat. She hugs the shoes to her chest.

The uncle speaks. "School is for boys."

Rashmina walks quickly to the door. She sits down in the yard. Her aunt comes outside, crouches beside her, puts her arm around Rashmina's shoulders.

"We will treat you well," she says, "like a daughter."

The boys appear at the door.

"You can play football with us," says the youngest one.

Rashmina puts her shoes down carefully.

"I don't like football," she says. "I like reading."

The cousins stare at her, shuffle their feet.

"I want to go to school. Please."

"I am sorry," says the aunt, "There is no money for you to go to school. Do not ask your uncle again."

Later, as daylight fades, Rashmina sits hugging her shoes. She longs for her mother, for her old home, for her school. Her aunt comes out, strokes her hair.

"You are safe with us, Rashmina." She ushers her boys away to bed.

The girl bites her lip. She looks up. A single aeroplane glints above her. One of Jhalak's skybirds, she thinks. She watches as the golden vapour trail stretches and fades. And disappears forever.

Then Rashmina stands up, and goes inside the house, leaving the sturdy black shoes stranded in the yard.

About Veronica

Veronica Bright loves creating stories, a skill which came in handy when she worked as a primary school teacher with delightful, bouncy, and exhausting 4 and 5 year olds. It was these children who inspired her to write stories, poems and plays, and were the first characters in the test runs of the bite-size dramas published by Kevin Mayhew as "Frogs in Assembly" and "Robots in Assembly".

Now retired, she writes short fiction, for which she has won a number of prizes, including a weekend at the Winchester Literary Conference, and a week at the Swanwick Writers' Summer School. Her short stories have appeared in numerous anthologies. Veronica runs the Plymouth Christian Writers' group, and also belongs to the Plymouth Proprietary Library Writers' Group. She appreciates the peace and quiet now that her children have left home, but welcomes interruptions from anyone bearing gifts of cups of tea and chocolate biscuits.

Veronica's latest stories may be found in Greenacre Writers Anthology Volume 2, published in 2013, Belper Arts Festival Short Story Anthology, published 2013, The Write Path 2013, National Association of Writers' Groups Anthology.

www.veronicabright.co.uk

Holes in the Blanket by Valerie Clements

Snug as a bug in a rug. My grandmother's words as she wrapped me in a blanket, pulling it securely round my shoulders. One of the treats when staying with her was sitting in the garden, warm and securely wrapped, under the midnight sky, watching the stars.

Holes in the blanket she said. For a small child, the idea that the stars I saw were holes in the blanket of night, through which we glimpsed the brightness of heaven was intriguing. The thought of night as a blanket appealed to me, the thick darkness as comforting and reassuring as the shawl around my shoulders. I was a child who was loved and indulged.

The night he proposed the stars shone brilliantly too. Walking home after a party, we paused to gaze at the winter sky, and he pointed out and named for me the familiar constellations, Orion, the Plough, the Twins. I was reassured by the confidence with which he guided me across the heavens. Finally he pointed to Rigel, shining blue-white in Orion's heel.

'That will be our star', he announced, 'and when we've been married fifty years, we'll say 'We fell in love under that star'.

The comfort of his voice, his presence, his certainty held me. That easy assumption of a settled future, tucked as securely around my shoulders as my childhood blanket.

Of course, as his career developed there was no longer time for walks under the stars. But the comforting warmth of the blanket remained. I lacked nothing. We moved from house to house, dream to dream. His dreams. Of course I gave up my job. I was his wife, wasn't I ? 'No-one can say that I can't provide for my family – no wife of mine will need to work.' Of course the children were perfect, bright, intelligent and beautiful. It was a pleasure to retreat into motherhood. We took holidays, entertained friends, built our future. Nothing was too much for him to organise. I wasn't even aware of the blanket being pulled higher; I only felt it being tucked tenderly under my chin. There was nothing to struggle against. Being with a confident, masterful man was a thrilling experience, to relax and allow him to take control, to make our decisions. After all, he had my best interests at heart, and I welcomed his care, felt cherished by his concern. I felt loved and indulged.

When he told me about the Chicago office, I panicked. I wept, sobbed, clung to him. But he was right, of course. A year in the States would enhance his standing with the company. It would broaden his outlook, widen his horizons. It would be foolish to uproot the children for the sake of one year. Chicago was no place to bring up children. They were too young to appreciate the experience. He was sure that I would not like it. He was leaving in a week.

So I washed, ironed, packed. I kept my terror to myself. The last morning I cooked a large breakfast. I wanted him to know I loved him.

'Just cereal and toast would have been better' he muttered. 'Do you want me to be uncomfortable on the plane?'

I hadn't thought. I felt ashamed of my stupidity. He kissed me briefly, said goodbye to the children and left. Long after the car had turned the corner, I remained on the doorstep. The simple act of closing the door behind him would commit me to the future. And I was afraid.

That first night going to bed was an ordeal. I checked the doors and windows, unplugged everything, then came downstairs and did it all again. In my panic I couldn't remember the alarm code; I was afraid that once it was set, I wouldn't be able to turn it off. So I left it. I felt overwhelmed by the responsibility for myself and the children. With the curtains firmly closed I lay awake in the darkness, tense and cold. Alone.

Next morning, business-like for the children's sake, I made breakfast, packed lunches, took the children to school. Somehow the day passed. And the next. No planes had crashed. It was on the third afternoon, returning with the children from school, I heard the phone as we walked up the path. My key jammed in the lock, and the ringing stopped before I could get in. I had let him down. Perhaps he was missing us, already homesick, and I had not been there for him. An hour later, he rang again.

'Don't worry.' He brushed aside my apologies. 'Forgot the time difference. Missing me?'

My tears started then, and I pleaded with him to come home.

'You're just being silly,' his tone was brusque. 'And selfish. How do you think hearing you cry makes me feel? I'll be home for Christmas, and I'll ring when I can. This is a great opportunity for me – do you want me to waste it?'

He was right, of course. It was only twelve weeks to Christmas. And I was a grown woman. I crossed off every day on the calendar, counting the days, waiting for him.

At half-term I took the children to buy new shoes, searching for the styles he had always bought for them. Sensible shoes. My daughter wanted red, but he thought red shoes looked cheap, so I had to refuse her. After all, it was his money. I wrote regularly, recounting all the details of home. He replied fitfully, scribbled notes with little details.

'Make up your own mind. Decide for yourself,' he replied when I asked his opinion. But I found that I was incapable. I wanted to please him, to keep everything, including myself, as he liked, but how could I when I no longer knew his preferences? The image I had of him was becoming blurred by distance.

I planned Christmas with care: his favourite foods, wines, cheeses. Buying a tree was difficult, and in the end the one I chose, although pretty, was not quite perfect, neither in shape or colour. Although I decorated it lavishly, I knew he'd notice its imperfections. And comment. On Christmas Eve he arrived late and irritable. The flight had been delayed. He discharged armfuls of packages, took off his coat and slumped into an armchair. I kissed the top of his head.

'Just pour me a drink, will you?'

He went to bed early, jetlagged and worn out by the journey. I filled the children's stockings myself.

The holiday passed quickly. He relaxed, joined in the children's games, visited friends. Took control. But he was bored, in the way that a caged lion is bored, seeming relaxed and lazy behind the bars, but with one ear listening for the key in the lock, the drawn bolt. The cage finally opened one raw January morning when he drove back to the airport. This time I closed the door with a faint sense of relief.

Spring came late. I had my hair cut. On impulse, but with no regrets. I was walking home with the shopping when the clouds parted and a shaft of late March sunlight warmed my shoulders. I felt old and worn out with trying.

'A new look' I told the hairdresser and surprised myself with the decisive note in my voice. It was a cliché, but true. He preferred my hair long and thick, twisted about his fingers. I didn't tell him.

As Easter approached the children needed summer clothes, and this time my daughter had her red shoes. It had been four weeks since I had heard from him. I had no phone number at which he could be reached. There had been no provision made for domestic catastrophes. Now there was no need. At night I slept soundly. When his letter came, three days before Easter, the pain was only momentary, not deep and piercing. He was too busy. There was a conference and important clients. He was sure I would understand. I did.

The children and I went to the seaside. A day-trip. I forgot the cagoules, and we ate fish and chips in a bus shelter, watching the rain. But it didn't matter. Not any longer. The children enjoyed themselves and so did I. I coped.

It was in May that I began to leave the bedroom curtains open. The stars winked at me, and the bed no longer felt cold and empty. I found I was looking forward to the summer. He no longer phoned, but in a rare letter he insisted that I book a cottage in Wales – a bolthole for him to recharge. He was ready for a break at home. There was no need for a holiday abroad, and a cottage would be relaxing. He was sure I could make it just like home.

The old panic returned, but accompanied this time by irritation. When the next letter came, I was ready. He was disappointed, but he'd been invited to spend summer on the Vineyard – business with pleasure, of course. He was sure that I'd understand. I did.

Perhaps that was one of the best summers I had ever known. The days were long and lazy. I slept deeply and rose early. I spent whole days in the garden, letting the grass grow, watching the clouds, dreaming. The house remained uncleaned, happily untidy. The children and I ran wild and free. I had cancelled the cottage. He had insisted that we go. I had decided otherwise.

The children no longer ask about their father. Only occasional comments, almost as afterthoughts. The strong sun of summer bleaches out everything, even memories, it seems.

I have started drinking tea again at breakfast. I realise that I never really liked the freshly-ground, freshly-percolated coffee of that other life. This morning the children have already left for school. The first

17

day of term no longer worries me. Now I cope. Responsibility for others and for myself is not a burden as I had been told. Only the blanket of his concern had become too heavy for my shoulders. But now that blanket is all in holes, and through those holes I can see the stars.

The last letter lies unopened. I will have my tea. He must learn to wait.

About Valerie

Recently retired, **Valerie Clements** finally has more time to follow her interests – raising herbs, textile art, singing with two local choirs, and canal boats. Her greatest passion, however, is and always has been, writing in one form or another. If asked to describe herself in just one word, she would be likely to say 'word-wrangler'

Throughout Valerie's working life she has handled and manipulated language to one degree or another – as a translator and co-editor of a Christian magazine for children, a lecturer in modern languages in further education ad, more recently, working with students with specific learning difficulties and disabilities. In that role she specialised in dyslexia support and transcribing text into Modified English for hearing-impaired students.

So far, Valerie's fiction output has been limited to a range of stories for her three grandchildren, although she is currently working on a Christian science-fiction fantasy novel for younger teenagers.

'Holes in the Blanket' is her first published work.

The Happening at Snarford by Margaret Davies

"Look at that magnificent hammer-beam roof. And the angel carvings, so characteristically East Anglian. The whole timber roof is typically English. There's nothing like it in Europe."

My mum gazes at The Nerd Geoffrey, as if he was the Angel Gabriel, come specially from Heaven to tell her this.

"It's amazing the things you know," she breathes. "So well-informed. I don't know how you do it."

It's perfectly obvious how he does it. He was reading the guide-book when we came into the church. But it's not obvious to my mother. She wants to admire The Nerd Geoffrey, set him on a pedestal.

If she'd been like that about my dad, they might still be together.

Subject closed. We had a colossal row, me and my mum. Slinging accusations at each other. "You're so self-centred" "What do you think it's like for me?" "You never think of me." Etc. We made up, sobbing in each other's arms, agreed we wouldn't argue again. But it won't be easy if mum keeps looking at The Nerd Geoffrey, eyes glistening like blobs of jam.

In a side-chapel, these two statues of people, lying on their backs on shelves, the man on the top one, wife below. They're dressed like in Shakespeare, ruffs round the neck. He's got on these padded breeches and looks a twit. She's wearing a gown with another ruff round the hips which sticks up in front. Must be uncomfortable to lie on. She's got this long stiff face, as if she thinks it's good being uncomfortable and whingeing is for wimps.

"Sir Geoffrey and Lady de Roylins, Lord and Lady of the manor in Tudor times." The Nerd Geoffrey sounds pleased with himself having the same name as this dead lord, as if it makes him a knight or something.

"Geoffrey," murmurs my mother. "There's something special about old names, a kind of nobility."

Sometimes I worry about her.

The Nerd Geoffrey smiles. "This Sir Geoffrey seems to have a noble character. He rebuilt the tower - paid for it and had a hand in designing it. A man of many parts."

I scoff at this old bilge but I've got an uncomfortable feeling about this place. Like when someone breathes down your neck and the bumps on your spine shiver.

"Sshh, someone's listening," I whisper, but they don't hear.

"See round the edge of the memorial - their many children."

I look at the statues and there are little figures of children along the edge of each shelf, boys dressed like their dad round the top shelf and girls in long frocks with sticky-out waists like their mum on the bottom one. I count five boys and seven girls.

Mum's looking at them stunned. "Twelve altogether. You wonder where they all fitted - that manor house wasn't very big."

"They wouldn't all have lived," says The Nerd Geoffrey casually. "Some would have died in infancy. That's why they had so many, to ensure some survived."

He knows everything - except he doesn't know that it's sad so many died. No wonder she looks a bit stiff. She'd have bawled her eyes out if she let herself.

"Her life would have been full," The Nerd Geoffrey tells my mother. "Her home, her children, her husband - being a helpmeet to him."

He smiles at mum and she - help - smiles back. I can't stand it.

Again I hear this breathy sound behind me and the knobs on my backbone poke through the skin. I turn quickly, suspecting TNG but he and mum have moved back into the aisle and they're looking up at the roof, mum's eyes spinning with vertigo.

"Come on, Sophie."

I'm right behind them. No one's leaving me in this creepo place.

Outside the sun feels good, but there's a nippy wind. Oh no, I've left my jacket in the church.   "Mu-um." I don't want to go back in there alone. But mum and TNG are in the graveyard, looking at the top of the church. "Awesome interweaving of art and technology." They're admiring Sir Geoffrey's creation.

I'll just gallop back, grab my jacket and be back here before I know I've gone. Zoom up the aisle. Where - ? Oh there on the floor, near the statues. Quick grab. Hell, fumbled it. Mustn't say hell in church. It's okay, no one to hear but me and Lord and Lady de Thingy.

Her eyes are on a level with mine, as I straighten up. The paint sits on the rough stone in little flakes. It's rubbed off in places. Maybe it's that gives Lady R a funny expression - as if she's just stopped doing something. As I watch, her top lip stretches, her chin drops and she yawns. Loudly. That's what I heard before.

"You - yawned," I say. My eyes saw and my ears heard but my brain is flashing: not possible.

Nothing happens. I tell myself I imagined it. I don't believe myself. Then this drawly, yawny voice says, "A tedious boring place. Nothing happens in Snarford. I thought you had gone. With those others, your parents."

"They're not my parents. Well, she's my mother. But The Nerd Geoffrey is not my father."

"Your father is dead?" She doesn't drip with sympathy. But she wouldn't. She's not exactly alive herself. I'm not going to think about this.

"No, but my parents have split."

She turns towards me. I wish she wouldn't. "Split?"

"Divorced."

She's impressed. I can tell by the way her heavy stone eyelids lift. "Divorced? Like the King? By Act of Parliament?"

"Erm, don't think so." She's thinking of Henry VIII - not very like my dad. "I should have been going out with him today (my dad, I mean, not the King) but he cancelled. I said he was a miserable git and mum got all worked up. We had a row about it." Why am I telling this old dame? She probably doesn't understand a word. But she listens.

Not like my mum who starts to shout as soon as I say anything. "You're not to talk like that, Sophie. It isn't that dad doesn't love you. It's just that sometimes grown-ups have to do things which means breaking other arrangements."

I wish she wouldn't say grown-ups as if I was a kid. I'm nearly thirteen, be a teenager next October. Boy, is she going to have problems then.

"The thing that gets me," I explain to Lady R, "is the way she sticks up for him when I know she doesn't mean it. I hear her shouting down the phone, giving him hell for letting me down. Then she comes to me as if I was deaf or stupid, 'It's not his fault, Sophie. These things happen.' I love my dad, but he is a miserable git sometimes."

She gives a sigh of satisfaction; hasn't had this much excitement since the last time the Spanish invaded. Must be a bit like watching East Enders in Serbo-Croat.

"Does he ever speak?" I jerk my head towards the shelf above. Does she know he's there? She wouldn't be able to see him unless she gets off her shelf and walks around. If she makes one move to get up, I'll be out of here so fast, I'll set a world record. "Sir Geoffrey," I add.

"Nay. He spoke a vast deal in life. His breath is used."

"Still, a man of many parts, hey?" I remember TNG's verdict. Lady R's forehead crinkles, deep stone waves with little pink flakes on them. I hope her face doesn't fall off.

"He built the church tower," I say.

"He? Nay, 'twas I. With money from my dowry on the death of Lord Hardynge, my father. I devised the pattern of vine and oak and the frieze of the hunt, and ordered it to be built of stone from Caen, brought by sea and river. Master Guisborne, the mason, built at my direction. I had been a widow then some twelve year."

A door slams and a voice calls, "Sophie. What are you doing? We're waiting for you."

"Just getting my jacket."

Mum appears, TNG behind her. "Come outside and look at the tower. There's a frieze round it, of a hunt. It's so clever."

"Renaissance man," says TNG with reverence.

"Renaissance woman, actually." I glance at lady R but her face is stiff again. "Lady de Roylins built the tower."

TNG smirks. "Sorry, Sophie, no women's lib in those days. She wouldn't have had the education. Having babies, looking after the house would be her level."

Do I hear another yawn? "Sir Geoffrey died in 1516." I can see this in the writing round the monument. "The tower wasn't started until 1528."

TNG shakes his head, looking amused. He glances at the church guide and the amusement falls off like little flakes. "Extraordinary," he mutters.

Mum puts her arm through TNG's and makes sympathetic noises. She smiles a secret smile to me over his shoulder, woman to woman.

Last glance at Lady R as I leave. Some of the red has lifted off her top lip, so the mouth has this little curl, like a smile.

About Margaret

I've been writing for years – short stories and novels. I've had a few stories published and am looking for an agent for my latest novel.

I read English at Kent University and King's College, London. I have worked in the public sector most of my career, most recently as Communications Officer for a drug and alcohol team. Now I'm retired I should, in theory, have more time to write – but it hasn't happened so far!

I'm a keen member of a writers' group and value the feedback I get there.

I love mediaeval architecture – castles, manor house and churches - and relish "gothic" stories that exploit these settings. I don't believe in ghosts but find they are a useful way of talking about human experience.

Fibonacci's Tree by Tracy Fells

'Here I am!' I jab a finger, one of the few that still works, at the notebook page. 'Right at the bottom of the tree.'

Tanya is adding too much milk to my tea. She doesn't think I'm looking when she shoves a custard cream into her mouth. It disappears whole like an envelope propelled through a gaping letterbox. Crumbs splutter across the back of my useless left hand as she chants, 'Teatime, Ellie. Sorry, we're out of custard creams, but I've saved you a Bourbon. They're your favourites.'

I can hear the words inside my head. They are crisp and clear like Mum's best crystal, singing out, perfectly formed in tone and pitch. 'My name is Eleanor and I loathe Bourbons, they are not proper chocolate biscuits.'

'Go on then, you can have two today.' Tanya's swollen pigeon bust almost knocks my glasses off as she bends forward to peer at the notebook. 'What you drawing? Oh, is that your family tree, Ellie? My brother's into all that, he's always on the Internet searching those family history sites you see on the telly.'

I steer my right index finger to the name adjacent to mine. 'Jacob, my brother, son of Harold and Kitty, he died a millennium ago, before the Falklands. Back in the day when a soldier dying overseas didn't make the news, it was expected – par for the course.' Retracting the shaking hand to the safety of my lap I stare at the chipped teacup, resolve to focus on the now and not slip backwards, out of time. 'I'm the last of the line, you see. Eleanor Palmer, the only living branch of the Palmer tree. The Palmers from Colchester, that is.'

Tanya's greasy finger streaks the white page. 'Is that you, Ellie? Eleanor Katherine Palmer, ain't that grand? Shame nobody uses names like that anymore. The world's got enough Sharon and

Tracey's, that's what I said to my Trish. I suggested Daisy, perfect name for her new little one, but she fancies Cheryl. Your own kids don't listen to sense, do they?'

Surely the woman can see the tree dies with me? I fell in love too late to sprout a Trish of my own. It was my own fault. I understood the theory of child bearing, analysed the mechanics and read all the manuals, even enjoyed the practical work but found I was long past the use-by date when it came to breaking eggs. Yes, I may be mixing my metaphors, but who cares. I'm eighty-six years old and can do what the hell I like, as long as it doesn't involve the left hand side of my body, which has buggered off to no-man's land on a permanent sabbatical. Except, I can't do anything - even with the working half. Can't pull up my own knickers without falling flat on my face. I have tried, but the last attempt ended badly with a broken nose and blood on the carpet. Sadly, I need both arms working to prise open the top floor window. Without two good legs I doubt I could climb out onto the fire escape anyway. Mercifully, my now second-rate brain is spared the dilemma of having to make the next decision in the chain: to escape down the fire escape, or plummet head first to oblivion? Most days I would choose oblivion.

'The tree is withered, old and dying, just like me,' I say loudly. 'They're all dead. Jacob. Mummy. Dad. Granddad Palmer. Nanna. Auntie May. Cousin Tilda. Uncle Mac. All dead.' A sudden thought makes me giggle. 'Death must run in the family. I'm the last in the line of corpses, descended from the dead!'

'Bed?' Tanya is picking out a chocolate digestive from the biscuit tin. 'No, Ellie, it's teatime not bedtime. After your cuppa I can push you outside for an afternoon snooze, would you like that?'

Another thought seeps into my retarding brain. The sparse branches of my family tree settle into a pattern across and down the page. If I squint out of my right eye I can decipher a sequence. Nature loves numbers and if you search long enough you can unravel the secrets of the universe. That's what Solomon Khan, my tutor and lover, taught me. 'God is a mathematician, can't you see that Tanya?' I snap at her then snatch up the pencil, still deliciously sharp, and wield it like a jousting lance.

She twitches, jumping back to clink against the tea trolley. 'Hey, now watch what you're doing with that, Ellie. You could poke someone's eye out.'

'There in the branches of the tree, just like the sequence of petals in a flower, can't you see the pattern?' The words are tumbling out like acrobats, but the woman stares stupidly at me, eyes as bulging as her navy blue uniform. I laugh as the solution appears; it's beautiful and elegant like a perfect equation. 'Fibonacci numbers,' I tell her. Isn't it obvious? 'I will call this Fibonacci's Tree!'

Tanya nods and smiles. 'Yes, poppet, it is a tree. Clever girl. Your family tree.'

I stick the pencil on a blank page of the notebook and carefully print out F-I-B-O-N-A-C-C-I. Underlining the name several times until the paper almost rips.

A gentle voice speaks up from behind me, a young, male voice. 'Ian wondered if you needed any help with the teas, Tanya?' Stooping slightly, he fidgets self-consciously as if he's cast himself as Gulliver in this strange land of wheel-bound gnomes. His slim, lanky limbs and pallid skin are the classic branding of student living.

Tanya sniffs. 'Thinks I need a chaperone now, does he?' She slips two Jammie Dodgers into her side pocket. 'I'll get round the old bats a lot quicker without a boy-scout tripping up the trolley.' Now she's whispering to me again. 'Summer students are a bleeding pain, Ellie. This one thinks he's Einstein, a right clever dick.'

'I don't think Ian would like you referring to the-' The poor lad stumbles, aware that I'm the gooseberry in their conversation.

'Inmates,' I offer.

'Guests,' says Tanya, relishing her sneer. 'Ian prefers us to treat and think of the old bats as guests, but then he's as batty as the best of them. Besides, Ellie here had a massive stroke and doesn't understand a word. She likes to sit and doodle, burbling away like a gargoyle.'

I like Tanya's image of a dribbling old gargoyle, it accurately describes the outward appearance of many of my fellow guests. Quite an imaginative turn of phrase for Tanya's tiny vocabulary, she must have overheard it.

Matt (I read his name badge as he leans towards the trolley) lets me choose a biscuit from the tin. My right hand does a circuit of the tin before digging out the last remaining chocolate Hobnob. He'll pay for this kindness later with a "bollicking" from Tanya in the staff quarters.

'Poor mare,' continues Tanya, 'can't even remember her name. Look she's drawing out her family tree and then scribbles Fibow-, Fibonacho or something. You wonder what's going on inside their heads.'

Matt stands close beside me and reads from the notebook. His spiked up hair smells of coconut. 'A lot is still going on inside Professor Palmer's head.' He pauses to smile at Tanya, a sweet boyish smile, which says so much more than his words. 'The name is Fibonacci. He was an Italian mathematician working in the thirteenth century. Devised a numeric sequence, also known as Fibonacci numbers or Fibonacci's Series. The sequence is found throughout nature in the arrangement of flower petals, or leaves on a tree or-'

Tanya holds up her hand. 'Yeah, that's great Matt, but I get enough gibberish from this lot without you joining in.' She waggles her wristwatch at him. 'Time for my fag break. You can finish up here.

And don't let them put their sticky mitts in the tin – you choose the biscuits.'

Once Tanya has slalomed through the sleeping guests in the conservatory and squeezed out into the walled garden, Matt pulls up a chair. 'Hobnobs are my favourites too, you want proper chocolate on a biscuit, don't you?' This time his smile is genuine. He has lovely blue eyes, bright and clear like a summer's day. For a nanosecond I allow myself to think of Solly. 'I've read all your books and papers, Professor Palmer. But I'm still struggling with your proof of Solomon's Theorem. I know it took you a lifetime to decipher and I've only been working on it for a year ...'

'Ah yes, but then I knew the inner workings of his mind. Solomon Khan was a great friend, you see.' I hesitate as his summer eyes begin to cloud. Not even the golden haired boy can understand my gargoyle gurgles, nobody can.

'I'm sorry,' he murmurs, 'I didn't catch all of that. Perhaps you could use your pencil. It's just ... may I ask you a question, Professor Palmer?' I nod, but also print out O-K on a new page of the notebook. 'I want to reference your proof in my dissertation ... it would great if you could look it over – the dissertation I mean. Would you do that for me?'

A sliver of spittle is trickling down towards my dimple; I try to swipe it away with my hand. Matt takes out a handkerchief, a proper one with his initials, and cleans my chin quickly. 'Thank you,' I say.

'There you go. Don't worry, Professor, I'm a terrible dribbler too. My girlfriend's always teasing that she can read the lunch menu from the stains on my shirt.'

I want to take his hand, but I know the care assistants are not encouraged to touch the guests and I've got him into enough trouble already. The notebook is slipping from my lap and I prop it up with the working knee. A pile of papers will be a disaster, I won't cope with his printed dissertation and I want to help him. I may never go to the loo on my own again, but I can tap on a keyboard and comment on Matt's work. I can be useful. Clutching the pencil I write: L-A-P-T-O-P?

'Would that help you?'

I nod and one side of my mouth is smiling.

'You can have my old laptop, Professor. I'll copy over my dissertation and bring it in tomorrow.'

Matt laughs as I give him the thumbs up, just the one. My lazy thoughts are whirring back to life. The laptop would be a communication tool; I could become the Stephen Hawking of Sunny Days Residential Home. I can tell Tanya to keep her thieving hands off the custard creams and share what I really think of her dreadful daughter Trish.

He returns to the trolley and unhooks the brake. Like a little boy Matt whispers from behind his hand, 'You must let me know if there's anything else I can do for you, Professor Palmer.'

I scribble one last message: CALL ME ELEANOR.

About Tracy

Tracy lives with her family close to the South Downs in West Sussex. In 2012 she was shortlisted for the Fish International Flash Fiction Prize, won the Steyning Festival Short Story Prize and the Choc-Lit Short Story Competition and has been shortlisted in numerous writing competitions. Her fiction has been published in Take-a-Break Fiction Feast, People's Friend, The Yellow Room, Rattle Tales2, Hysteria1 and The New Writer. Non-fiction features have been published in Writing Magazine.

Currently she is working on a novel and has started an MA in Creative Writing at Chichester University. Tracy has written several short plays, one of which was long-listed in the 2013 Kenneth Branagh Drama Award, and is currently writing a radio drama.

Several of her stories are available for download from Alfie Dog (alfiedog.com/products-page/tracy-fells/), Tracy shares a writing blog with The Literary Pig (tracyfells.blogspot.co.uk/) and tweets as @theliterarypig. She is actively involved in West Sussex Writers and loves meeting other writers to talk shop.

Proof by Sarah Hegarty

I'm walking so quickly I'm level with the van before I see it, parked at the end of the street I cross every morning. My chest pinches and I slow down. I can't see the number plate, but it's definitely his. In the April sunlight the blue spray job looks even crappier. If I went round the front, I'd see the wing dent where he hit the wall the night he left.

It's parked outside a gone-to-seed Victorian three-storey. There's a basement too, I notice through the railings. There'll be plenty of work: new windows, kitchen, bathroom; maybe knocking down walls and ripping out chimneys. Then all the decorating. There'd have to be a deposit for materials. And the bill settled in full, within seven days. I used to insist on that.

But insisting only got me so far.

He always ended up working Saturdays, because the job was over-running, and the customer threatening not to pay. And on Sundays he wanted to tile the bathroom, or sand the stairs, or change the kitchen cupboards.

'We should have bought shares in these,' I used to say, as I slashed the top off yet another microwaveable TV dinner.

As I approach the van the barking starts. I'm not surprised. He always got what he wanted. I peer through the back window. Standing on a blanket, surrounded by old paint tins and lengths of wood, is a scrappy little terrier, dirty white, missing an eye. Obviously been in a few fights.

I stare in at the familiar mess, and the pathetic little dog defending its territory. It leaps up and growls at me. There's manky, stretched skin where its right eye should be. It doesn't look very lovable.

'Just shut up, for Christ's sake!' I press my nose to the glass. 'Stop going on!' I'm glad when it throws itself around, snarling and yapping.

No worries, I'm off.

But as I'm walking past I turn, and look through the windscreen.

And then I can't help it. I lean into the van, which makes the dog even angrier.

I know how you feel, I want to say.

I get to work, and let myself in to the office.

I leave the answering machine on, and sit at my desk, staring at the archive shelves; at the rows of legal textbooks and folders, bursting with documents. All those words: all those voices. Who said what, to whom? Was the crime intentional? Accidental? Here's the evidence, Your Honour. Any mitigating circumstances?

Sometimes the wrong people get off, scot-free. When does 'no' turn into 'yes'? 'Never' slide into 'maybe'? How do you know when someone's lying?

He said we'd always agreed on it.

I said things change.

He said No meant No.

Someone will be in soon. I wander round and open the blinds, turn on the PCs and the shredder, and check the levels in the water cooler. I mark off another day on the Year Planner. At the top of the 'Live Cases' board, I rub out yesterday's date, and write in today's. But my fingers are wobbly. I have to do it twice. And then I feel my eyes stinging. I sit down quickly.

'Jane is the backbone of our admin team,' my last appraisal said. 'Always willing to cover for colleagues on leave.'

I'm fine once they've left. It's the weeks before that I can't stand: first the coy hints; then the endless discussions about cravings and clothes. All too soon, they're back; full of smug smiles and fake complaints, and moaning about lack of sleep. After a few minutes of it I have to get up and go to the Ladies.

I don't know why I kept a photo. Incriminating evidence, as our briefs would say. My fingers find it in my drawer, underneath a pile of recycled envelopes.

It's the seafront, at Brighton, three years ago. A bright Spring day. His birthday. I thought it would be the perfect surprise. But my timing's always been a bit dodgy.

We could get to the coast in a couple of hours, the van rattling, motorway slipping by like shed skin. We were off on an adventure; we were Bonnie and Clyde, we were invincible.

He'd rigged up an MP3 player on the dash, with the speakers in the back, and he played Springsteen. We were rolling down the highway, 'black top melting in the hot sun', even though I didn't know what 'black top' was, and it was never that hot. In Springsteen-land it was always summer.

But the van kept breaking down. And the middle safety belt didn't work.

'When are you going to get this fixed?' I used to say every time I got in, flipping the loop that hung down the back of the seat between us.

'I'll get round to it.' He was always fiddling with the music player when he should have been concentrating on the road. 'What's the problem? These two work fine.'

We'd just parked up, and were walking along the prom. He stopped and leaned on the railings, looking down over the beach. He was only wearing jeans and his old grey hoodie, and the wind was messing his hair, but he grinned at me, and my heart squeezed. Suddenly I wanted a photo of him. I don't know if he didn't hear me, or thought I'd already taken it, but he turned away at the wrong time.

The photo shows the back of his head. It's a good reminder.

I waited till we got to the pub. I thought it might be better somewhere contained: a cosy corner, just the two of us. Afterwards I wondered if I should have told him when we were walking on the beach, so the wind whipped our words away; so I didn't have to see the look on his face.

I knew how it'd happened, of course: I just couldn't believe it. It was Bank Holiday weekend, and the GP's was closed. I'd meant to find the duty chemist but I'd kept forgetting.

I saw something in the paper the other day, on the Women's Page: women these days are too ambitious; we want everything. We're making men nervous, undermining their confidence, wanting the same as them at work. At home, we're putting them under too much pressure to have the perfect relationship.

But I didn't want everything.

He said he'd come with me but I wanted to go on my own. Funnily enough I got my own way over that. I was pretty sure I knew what would happen. I just never thought I'd be doing it.

It was a largeish room, where you had to wait. Three rows of chairs, all facing forward. Pale walls. Net curtains that could have done with a wash. No one crying, luckily. I noticed an older woman, who'd brought a friend with her. The teenager along from me was definitely with her mum. She went in ahead of me, then came out again, and they sat whispering over a list of pros and cons. That's what the counsellor had suggested doing, if I had any doubts.

I didn't need a list. If I chose one, I had to lose the other. And it was still early: it was going to be straightforward.

Except it wasn't. There were some signs of deterioration, the lovely doctor said. It might just be me: how I was made. It might be to do with my age. I needed to be aware of it, for the future.

That was the bit I couldn't forget.

For a few weeks he insisted we went out on a Sunday: walks and pub lunches, or to the cinema if it was raining.

One overcast afternoon we were dragging up a hill towards an old church. The walking book said there was a great view from the graveyard at the top. Ahead of us was an older couple, with a light brown dog which kept circling them, looping backwards and forwards. It ran up to us, sniffing round our legs, and jumped up. I stood still, waiting for it to stop. But he bent down to it; patted its head, stroked its back. He laughed, and let it lick his hand. I watched its slobbering pink tongue on his wide fingers and I felt my eyes sting. I wanted to kick the stupid animal.

After it ran off, he said, 'Maybe that's what we need.'

'I don't want a dog,' I said.

Three months later he was in such a hurry to leave he drove the van into the front wall.

'There's no one else,' he said, 'there's only you.' But we wanted different things.

Even though I'd tried to want what he wanted.

I believed him. I always did.

But I didn't see what was staring me in the face.

I look at the photo again – really look at it, this time: at the back of his head, turned away. Already gone.

I get up, cross the room and carefully line the picture up on top of the shredder. Then I feed it into the machine.

No turns into yes, sometimes; sometimes it turns into maybe. Nothing stays the same forever.

And people can be wrong – even lovely doctors.

I sit at my desk, remembering my morning; remembering why I was walking so quickly, so confidently into the new day. I find my phone in my handbag. I start to tap out a text but that's not what I want. Instead I listen to the ringing tone. I'm about to press End when I hear the familiar voice.

'Hi, love. Everything okay?'

Because it hasn't been. Because for some women it will always be harder than for others.

In that one question I hear the depth of his concern. 'Yes. Yes, I'm fine.'

And I am.

It doesn't matter any more: the van with the dent; the barking dog; even the little blue and yellow checked car-seat, strapped in the front.

I can prod my heart, and it doesn't even twinge.

'I just wanted to – to tell you.' I fiddle with my wedding ring.

'Yeah?'

'Today – I – it's the first morning I haven't been sick.'

'Hey!' I can hear his smile. 'That's brilliant, Janey! Great! That's a good sign.'

I sit back in the chair and feel my shoulders relax. I picture him, hear his easy laugh.

'Yes.' I smile too. 'Yes, it is.'

About Sarah

Sarah Hegarty was born in Bristol, and grew up in the north-west. After graduating in Mandarin from Leeds University she worked as a print journalist, latterly as a freelance. She left journalism to start a family and studied for an MA in Creative Writing at Chichester University. Her short fiction has been published by Cinnamon Press, *Mslexia,* the *Momaya Annual Review* and on the web, as well as placed in competitions.

Her story *Something Hidden* is the title story of the forthcoming anthology from Bridge House. Her first novel, *The Ash Zone,* based on her experience of life in Beijing, won the 2011 Yeovil Literary Prize. She is one of the mentees on the 2013 Jerwood/ Arvon mentoring scheme, and is working on her second novel. She lives in Guildford with her family. www.sarahhegarty.co.uk

Kinder Surprise by Sheila Llewellyn

Ruby and I used to go on holiday together and we always, but always, ended up with seats on the plane near a wh-a-a-ah baby. 'Why don't they dope them?' I'd say, loud enough to make Ruby nervous. 'Or have separate baby flights where you can post them like cargo and pick them up at the other end?'

Ruby used to say, 'You'll change your tune one day. You'll want kids. I bet you get a wh-a-a-ah baby. You deserve one, the way you carry on about them.'

'Not me,' I'd say. 'No babies ever. Not the baby type.'

Ruby and I got to be thirty, still going on holiday together, still chasing the big career.

I got mine, she got the wh-a-a-ah baby. God help us, could that baby wh-a-a-ah.

'Much more of this,' she said, at the six month stage, coochy-cooing at this screeching open-stretched mouth in a Gap cap, 'much more of this, and mummy will have to send you back, YES - SHE - WILL.'

We both laughed, but the dark circles under her eyes, the mouth beginning to turn down with disappointment – I wasn't sure if she was joking or not. And I couldn't work out whether it was just the baby she'd send back or Andy the Horizontal Man – doer of the deed – as well.

'At least he stood by me,' she'd say, when I tackled her about settling for him. I never saw him standing much, he was more of a sofa type. Poor old Rube. Two wh-a-a-ah babies she ended up with, if you ask me.

We lost touch.

So she never got to meet baby Rupert. He was a little treasure. Still is.

After all I said about them, where did Rupert, my little Kinder Surprise, come from, then?

I reached forty. There I was in a Singapore hotel – exotic holidays on my own were by then a prerequisite to get through Christmas – and it was my last morning, kept free for shopping.

I woke up – and I was lonely. Not the no-one-on-the-pillow-next-to-me sort of lonely – a swift get up, a swim in the pool and a room service breakfast usually numbed that. More the so-miserable-I-was-unable-to-move-so-I-just-lay-there-heavy-limbed-and-helpless sort of lonely.

'You look sad, mum.' That's Rupert. He's lying on the sofa at the moment, looking at me.

'Just thinking about what it was like before you came along, pet.' Actually, I really have to work hard to remember what it felt like to be that lonely.

'Do you want a hug?' he says. And he comes across and wraps his arms round my neck and plonks a sloppy kiss on my cheek. Takes himself back to the sofa. Job done.

And I am back to thinking about Singapore. Christmas Day. Rupert Day. I'd managed to drag myself up and while I was waiting for breakfast, I'd got connected. Found a site I'd been checking out for some time. Just for the great graphics. Kind-a-Kinder.com. I scrolled down and there, enclosed in a tiny egg-shaped dot, was adorable, irresistible, updatable Rupert, aged zero. Perfect. One joining fee and as many apps as you like. I chose a 1:1 ratio – one real time month equals one virtual year. That meant it'd only take me one real time year to catch up with Ruby and her wha-a-a-ah baby. Rupert was waiting for me when I got home. The technical bit of him, that is. Large-framed glasses with a built-in screen operated by pressing the tiny gilt KK logo on the rim, wireless connection to an iPod look-a-like handset. Log on. Instant baby. Cool.

When he was a babe in arms, he was just suspended there in space in front of me, but on his second birthday, two months later, I treated myself to the new all-round vision they'd developed – just as well, because he was into everything and forever toddling off out of range, the little rascal.   He was a brilliant baby. All the baby books tell you a set routine is essential, so there was a short period of adjustment while I tried out various options, but remarkably little fuss once I set up the correct preferences for my particular lifestyle. Fantastic sleeper, he was then, straight through.

I can't tell you what it felt like to wake up to the morning alarm followed straight away by the gurgles and the goo-goos and the na-na-nas clicking on.

It's amazing the pleasure you get from even the most mundane things. I loved burping him. It made me feel really appreciated. I'd walk him up and down, stroking his back, and murmur to him and feel oh so close. I even pressed the sicky-up app once. I was wearing my work suit and the need to see what it felt like just took hold of me - to be in a rush to get to work then – oops! That oozy, soury, sicky-up experience! At last, I could hold my head up with the rest of the working mums in the office. Kept it to myself, of course. I didn't think they'd understand.

Mind you, once was enough for the sicky-up app. I know, I know, I could have put a towel over my shoulder and turned the sniff function off, but still. I also discarded the crappy app and the pappy app – choosing to change nappies? I don't think so. And what's the point of downloading a dad? He'd only get in the way.

The gappy app sounds good. For the future. Rupert can go anywhere, do anything. If he ever gets into difficulties, I just download the 'rescue' programme and home he comes. A fun gap year for him, none of the usual worry for me. They're continually updating the gappy app – who knows what might be available when he's ready for it? It could be the making of him.

We had a great time with the terrible twos. Took full advantage of the 'supermarket squeal' option, specially developed for maximum effect in enclosed spaces. A hot key allows you to project the squeal to about twenty yards away–simply press and enjoy. Everyone without children looks round, scowling; mums and dads look guilty then relieved when they realise it's someone else's child, but they end up scowling with everyone else because they can't locate the culprit, and if they can't locate the culprit, they can't feel superior.

'This is such fun, mama,' Rupert would say, and more times than not, we'd key it in again when boredom set in at the checkout. I think I spotted another Kind-a-Kinder.com mum in the supermarket recently – someone's squealer option was definitely on somewhere. I peeked down the aisle and there she was, wearing the KK Sunshades alternative design, I'm sure of it. But she took them off when she saw me staring at her and put them in her bag.

It was a bit difficult when Rupert was due to start school, last September, I don't mind admitting. I couldn't bear the thought of losing him. All those afternoon walks in the park, picking up autumn leaves then taking them home and drawing round them. All those mum and toddler swimming lessons: his face, panic stricken, as he doggy-paddled frantically towards me –

'Don't leave me mama, don't l-e-a-ve me!' I just wasn't ready to let go of all those together times, or share him with anyone else, like teachers, or – though I'm ashamed to say it – even share him with other little Kind-a-Kinder-Friends on the yappy app.

So, I re-loaded him. Twice. Back to being four. Old enough to have a conversation with, but young enough to think he's only got me in the whole wide world. I've no regrets. They're so precious, those baby-toddler-little man years. But you can't keep them like that for ever, can you?

Although, I was tempted. When he got to be five again, we were sitting having our birthday tea, and he looked so sweet, it did cross my mind to re-load just once more to four, but he looked at me and he said, 'I want to go to school, mama, I really do. I love you, but I want to go to school.'

I don't know where he got all that from, it's not in any app I've downloaded. And the tears didn't just roll down his cheeks, they splashed over his bottom eyelids and gushed. On reflection, I think I chose the wrong distress option. The 'tears in a torrent' preference was too much to bear. I managed to change it to 'tears in a trickle' but even a few tears are enough to break my heart.

Now here we are, and he's just had his eleventh birthday. I think that's brought on all this reminiscing – Rupert reaching another milestone. And there's a little problem we're going to have to work through together. I've been made redundant. Surplus to requirements, they said, but I've had quite a lot of sick leave recently and I guess that hasn't helped. I haven't been sick, of course.

I just played the system so I could have as much time off as I could to be with Rupert. It's been worth it though, this extra time. We've grown closer. I very rarely put him on stand-by. I know it'll be difficult when he goes to secondary school. I had his name down on the

Indie-app for one of the good Independents, but it's not going to happen now I'm out of a job. I've only just summoned up enough courage to tell him.

He's been lounging on the sofa all this time since the sloppy kiss, working his way through his birthday presents. So I go across to him, stroke his hair back from his face and tell him about the school finances problem. He looks at me, unblinking. Seems to last an age. I think for a moment he's frozen up, and I'm about to try a soft reset, then he shrugs and smiles with one side of his mouth. He's having to grow up so fast, my little man. It's the first discussion we've had about life's disappointments. I'm so overcome, I have to log him off for a moment and de-mist my glasses.

It crosses my mind to slow him down again, maybe reload him, just a year back. Shield him a little longer, the finances might get better. But he's already had a growth spurt and a super-tall ten year old might have problems – children can be so cruel. It wouldn't be fair on him. So I put the glasses on again and fetch him back to me. He's still lying on the sofa, but he looks up and waves, his little face sunny and carefree once more. Looks like he's already learning to deal with the ups and downs of real life. I'm so proud of him.

'Come over here, Mama.' Mama. Like he's four again. Irresistible.

'Just coming, darling,' I say, adjusting his brightness a little as I make my way across.

'I'm so sorry about the school thing, I really am,' I say, me hugging him this time.

'You promised me only the best, mother. You promised,' he says, giving me a thoughtful look as he pushes me gently away. Then he turns his High Definition smile full on, and passes me the phone he's been playing with. The one he wanted for his birthday.

I check out the screen.

MamaApps.com. And he's chosen 'Rock Star, Rich as Croesus', as the default option.

We gaze at each other, worlds apart, our thumbs poised.

And I cannot bring myself to press Delete.

About Shelia

I worked overseas for fifteen years for the British Council and for other institutions. Then I retrained as a psychologist specialising in Post Traumatic Stress Disorder, and came to live and work in Northern Ireland ten years ago. I took early retirement five years ago and began to concentrate on my writing. In 2011 my radio drama won the P.J. O' Connor Radio Drama Award and was broadcast on RTÉ One, and then went on to win a Silver Award at the New York International Radio Festival. Over the past two years, I've been shortlisted for several competitions, including the Bridport Prize, the Seán Ó 'Faoláin Short Story Prize and the Costa Short Story Prize.

I'm now studying for a PhD in Creative Writing at the Seamus Heaney Centre at Queen's University Belfast.

Mirrorland by Margaret McAlister

It began as a game you played when you were alone in your room. I would walk in to find you pressed up to the glass, peering intently into dimly lit vistas and impossible distances that only you could see. It was a world far beyond your own reflection and the inverse image of your candy pink bedroom. You weren't looking at yourself but at something far away, far out of reach. I imagined a world of fairy gardens and enchanted woods, of tooth fairies with their spidery mirror writing. I imagined shifting shadows and whispered secrets, and castles shimmering in the moonlight. I imagined a world of mystery and adventure, of dark promises, glinting silver and starlight.

You're such an imaginative child. You populate your world with invisible companions, angelic visitors. You scatter cushions on the floor and stride oceans and rivers, your giantess legs taking you across ice caps and continents. For a child who cannot walk anywhere but dances and skips, it was a small imaginative leap for you to spring Alice-like through the looking glass and find a whole new world.

"It so closely looks like my room, mummy, and yet it isn't. It's completely different."

You then began to tell me that you could see your sister in the mirror and she would speak to you when nobody was looking.

You would call for her, not by name but by your relationship, 'Sister! Sister!' And I would pick up your laundry, fold your clothes and leave you in peace. You seemed excited and happy and I was pleased you had a sense of her, a special relationship.

You told me she lived in the mirror, and that you could play with her in Mirrorland. Sometimes she would come out and be naughty and once when I found black marker pen scribbled all over your white drawers, you cried and told me 'Sister did it!' I couldn't tell you off for it. Of course we both knew it wasn't true.

You saw her constantly in Mirrorland, the little sister you never met. You also told me about other things, about how Grandma would only ever use her walking stick indoors in Mirrorland, and never outdoors. When you started to lose your milk teeth I sat for hours writing tiny notes in backwards writing, and you would waken to hold them up to the mirror, slowly spelling out the words, magical messages promising pearl crowns, ivory cribs, enamel stools. Mirrorland was where the tooth fairies lived and you delighted over the silver coins they left you, refusing to part with them. Even now they have pride of place on our mantelpiece, gathering dust. You told me when you couldn't sleep, you sometimes went to play in Mirrorland. You said you would both pretend to be babies and listen to nursery rhymes.

You only asked to see her once, and it was the only time I lost control. It was the day before the burial and you were upset and couldn't understand why you wouldn't be able to see her just one time. I think you imagined her like a sleeping baby lying in a cot. I had just spent the whole afternoon with the doctors going through the post mortem report, every organ interrogated, prised open. There were no answers except the words macerated ... inconclusive. You had no idea what you were asking me. Every tiny part of her had been opened and examined and there were no answers, no explanations, no promises of pearl crowns or silver coins. Her Moses basket was a wicker coffin. She had come too soon, gone too soon. There were no comforting letters.

What was once a life inside me became a death inside me. I carried her for two days waiting to go into hospital to give birth to a death. The doctors were filled with pity when the wails broke out of my body, and I silenced them. It was an earth shattering silence, echoing the new stillness inside me, the heartbeat gone. So that day when you asked to see her, I had only wanted to remember her as I had last seen her, the tiny curved smile. The doctor crossed her arms and we had time to look at her. Her eyes still open, unseeing. The tiny umbilical cord, the beautiful shoulders, the small strong back. The knees together, legs falling to the side, like Christ on the cross. She was perfectly formed, cradled in the palm of my hand. All my dead hopes bundled up into the persistence of the possible, the devastating loss of what might have been.

You told me that a dog said meow and a cat said woof.

And they called black white and they called white black.

A pig was mud and mud was a pig.

Everything was opposite in Mirrorland.

After the post mortem came the homicide inquiry. What had I done to cause such a disaster? I became both the victim and perpetrator, flinching from the judge and expert witnesses who dredged up every wrong doing, mounting malicious attacks and apportioning blame. If only I had … what if I had … we endlessly re-create the past that is possible, but un-true. Things can't just be random and meaningless. I knew that if only I hadn't … the outcome would have been better, or what if I had … it all would have been different. And all the while the inescapable reality that it had happened, was happening.

Every wish has an unknown price to be decided by the fairies.

And how I wished for you, my own darling Joy. Your name came to me as a growing certainty as your budding life filled me and shone out of every pore. In my own Mirrorland you were my completion, the child I saw as my crowning joy. Even in my palms you were perfect and sanctified. Father Christopher poured holy drops of chrism oil on your tiny head and we blessed you.

Wallpaper was outside

51

And inside, gardens and trees.

Flowers grow in clouds and

It rains petals and daisies.

Stars live in the sea and the sun is the moon.

And they say words that don't really make sense in Mirrorland.

How could I make sense of it? Those words from the sonographer I never thought to hear? "I'm really sorry. It's not good news." I got up from the bed and walked across a room to my handbag to pick up my phone. I got up from the bed and walked across a barren wilderness, the surface of a dead moon. My husband's voice was a tiny signal from another universe and I sat weightlessly waiting for him to cross eternity to reach me.

One day you said in a low, confiding voice, "You know mummy, it's alright really because I actually didn't want another baby". I loved your childish honesty, the beautiful innocence of it. But I also knew you grieved the thought of a little sister and when we went to buy you a new bed, you wanted the bunk beds, mourning what might have been, the little sister sleeping below you. Then one night you had a nightmare and I ran in to find you sleepwalking, beating your hands against the glass. Trying to escape your monsters, you thought your mirror was your bedroom door and you were trying to get out. It broke my heart to see you so distressed and I also saw myself in you. How often do our hands beat against the cold unbreakable glass that separates us forever from the previous moment, the moment before the disaster, before the car crash, before the bad news, the shipwreck, the heart attack, the accident, the tsunami? And yet that moment lives on as the un-lived life, in an illusory world of what ifs, the better world that haunts us through the looking glass when alternatives to reality fail us. Trying to get back to that perfect moment, in search of Joy, I recklessly walked through every door that would open to me, until eventually I came to the door that led out of my marriage. As if the word marriage was too close to miscarriage, the blood bath of that delivery suite. I only wanted my own deliverance.

I entered my own Mirrorland, gazing Potter-like into my own Erised, trying to re-find the unlived life inside me. Small moments of regret haunted me, suddenly pregnant with meaning and loss. I remembered the time during the aftermath when we stayed in a beach house in Whitstable. We were suspended between the elements, the fertile fields stretching behind us for miles and the brown line of the estuary before us, silted with mud. Seagull cries filled the sky and tiny sparrows flew in and out between the beach huts feeding their nests. We were alone with the salty wind, stranded from our former lives like the old wooden boats upturned in the long grass, abandoned yet still hopeful. During our beachcombing we found a huge, perfect oyster lying in the shingle, and I wondered at the secret life inside it, a perfect pearl sealed tight against the light. We had been too afraid to eat it, and in the fading afternoon we tossed it back into the waves. A simple thing, that oyster, and yet how I came to mourn it, that careless casting away.

And I remembered the bigger things, the what ifs of previous lovers, the one who promised me the moon, the one who saw me as his perfect symmetry. And like the moon I borrowed my light, giving back only a reflection of what others wanted, hiding my darkness, my loss. Yet still you always anchored me, mooring me to the present and what was most real and alive. I stopped chasing shadows as your own life began to reclaim me.

We slowly re-entered time, and Joy became less imagined and more real. We let her go, returning her back to where she came from, and I knew we had arrived at last when you imagined her playing the cymbals in a Pink Floyd track as we blasted it out in the car, singing at the top of our lungs. Now I am able to place my hand against the cool glass of reality, touching only the meaningfulness of what simply is. We can hold the newborn babies of our friends, delighting in their fat hands as they grab fistfuls of air, grasping at life. Their grip is strong. And I remember that you also told me that Wonderland is next door to Mirrorland.

Years have passed, and now your mirror reflects back the image of yourself and your room, and when you look into it you see your own reflection. You love to dress up and pretend to be a vampire or a pirate and the mirror offers you back yourself, but utterly transformed. You play with lipstick and pirate scars and see only yourself, yes altered, but unchanged. You hesitate between outfits, loving the freedom of dressing yourself, unable to make the choice between sunhats, your baseball cap or straw trilby?

And you laugh and tell me, "Mirrorland doesn't really exist mummy. It's just a fake place I made up."

And in these bright Summer days, I watch you as you stream ahead of me through the long grass, dancing and skipping as the soft air kisses your palms. And I smile and shade my eyes as you fly towards your future, every golden part of you alive in the midday sun, and as solid and shining and real.

About Margaret

Maggie McAlister is a Jungian Analyst and Forensic Psychotherapist. She has written and published extensively in her professional field, but 'Mirrorland' is her first published work in fiction. The idea for Mirrorland was largely inspired by Daniel Kahneman's Nobel Prize winning work on 'Counterfactual Thinking' and the ways in which we attempt to undo reality to a past which is possible but untrue.

She has a background as an Arts Psychotherapist and has worked in forensic psychiatry for over seventeen years, specialising in psychotic violence. She lives in North London with her daughter.

The Majorelle Garden by Lynne Voyce

A Study of New Love in the Majorelle Gardens, Marakesh

A young woman stands on the brick red path that leads to what was once the art studio, the cobalt blue of the walls ahead a vivid contrast to her yellow hair. She wears a short, white cotton dress, showing her tanned limbs gleaming in the vivid sunlight. She is looking ahead of her as if she is about to embark on a journey. Her half smile and the fact her head is held quite high, gives the impression that she is aware of being viewed, either by us, the viewer, or by the other figure in the painting.

To the right of the picture is a man, he is dressed in a white djellaba; its hood is down. His hair gleams black in the sun and as with the woman we can see him in profile. He has a strong Arab nose and hollow cheeks. He is kneeling, looking at her from a distance. At first he appears to be kneeling in prayer but when we look closer it is to pick up a scatter of papers, perhaps to represent that he is a guide.

That there is no one else in the picture, in a public garden, suggests two things: first, that the painter has framed what we see to include just two of them, emphasising the connection they feel; and second, that they can only see each other in the gardens. Further, the glimpse we catch of the crucifix the young woman wears around her neck and the detail that the man is wearing subha beads, or Islamic prayer beads, means we are shown that there is a difference in culture and religion. But it also suggests that the viewer is intended to be of the woman's culture as there are no figures painted in traditional Islamic art. This could connote that at this stage in the relationship the young man is the one who most has to adjust to a new way of life and that he will be most judged for falling in love.

The sun is high in the azure sky. The quality of light shows it is high summer. The use of colour in the garden is deliberately spectacular against the white clad figures. Bright lemon, orange and aquamarine painted earthenware pots with verdant green leaves springing from their mouths line the ochre paths. Cactii thrust, phallic, into the sky, in varying shades: olive, pea, peacock. And at the top of the canvas we can see the fringe of the bamboo wood and the palm trees. But this study belongs to the young woman and the man.

A Study of Domestic Life in Birmingham, England

We see the room as if we are standing in it. It is a living room with a door open to the outside. Through the door we can see a bright green lawn, the edge of a copper beech tree and in the distance a child's swing. Inside the room is a settee against the wall, on it lies a woman in a sleeveless lime green dress, her arm trails on the floor and we can see the edge of a wedding band on her finger; her legs spill over the arm of the settee and are crossed at the ankle. Her feet are bare. Her face is turned to us but she is looking at a child playing on the rug in front of her. Her hair is pulled back and her face is clear of make up but is slightly tanned. She is smiling.

The floor is strewn with toys: an aeroplane, building blocks and coloured pencils. The room appears happily chaotic and messy. The child wears just a nappy and an amber tee shirt. Its sandy coloured hair is cut short, which suggests the child is a boy. His limbs are plump and tawny.

In the corner is an arm chair. At the foot of the chair are a pair of leather sandals, the size intimates that they belong to a man and over the back of the chair is a man's Mac.

On the walnut side board, amongst photo frames and a vase of pale pink chrysanthemums is an elaborately painted tagine, a Moroccan cooking pot. It appears deliberately incongruous. The fact it is in the living room suggests it is no longer used to cook with.

A Study of Loss in Birmingham England

This is a companion piece to the previous picture, as it appears to be set in the same room. The still open door reveals pale grass strewn with beech leaves, while we can make out the bare branches reaching into a pale sky. It is autumn. What is notably absent, however, is the swing.

Inside the room, sitting on the armchair is a man. The man we saw in the first study: 'New Love in the Majorelle Garden'. He wears a black djellaba, with the hood up, he holds a leather bound book and entwined in his clasped fingers are prayer beads. On his left hand the beads lie over a wedding ring. His head is bent and we can simply see his profile emerging from the rim of the hood. His face is unsmiling and he stares at the floor. His feet are bare.

Across the room, leaning against the sideboard is the woman from the previous two pictures. She too is wearing black, a tightly fitting skirt and jacket. Her stockings are black and her black patent shoes seem formal for a domestic scene. There is also a book in her hand, perhaps the Bible. She gazes absently at the papered wall ahead of her; the silver palm print is shimmering and ghostly in the weak light. Among the photographs on the sideboard, by the empty vase is a bottle of what appears to be liquor and a glass. If we look closely, we can see a lip stick mark on the glass, the same shade that the woman is wearing.

The figures are across the canvas from each other. The fact they are so far apart and facing in different directions signifies an emotional distance.

There is very few signs of a child in the room: the toys from the previous picture are gone and the room is neat and tidy. By the door, however, is a small pair of child's shoes. This suggests that the child, in some respect, has departed. The sombre nature of the light and mood of the piece means we could conclude the child is dead.

A Study of Loneliness Birmingham, England

This picture completes the domestic tryptich, set in Birmingham. We are in the same living room as in the previous two paintings. The room is bare but for furniture and a single photo frame on the sideboard. The glass in the frame shows the reflection of the open door, so we cannot discern who the picture is of. The tagine, with its bright colours, is absent.   There is no trace of another human being inhabiting the room: the toys and male clothing from the previous two pictures are completely gone. The children's shoes by the door, however, continue their eerie presence. Through the open door we can glimpse branches edged with rime, the frost hardened garden and a grey-white sky. It is mid winter.

This time the woman is in the armchair. She is alone in the room. In fact, there are no external signs of any one else. The woman wears a grey tweed skirt and a grey jumper, her face is impassive and composed. She sits upright, legs crossed at the ankle and her hands in her lap; the right is over the left so we cannot see a ring. Her hair and her skin also have an ashen tinge. Her expression is sombre. On the arm of the chair we see a torn envelope and an open letter.

This picture is strongly connected to the first, 'New Love in the Majorelle Garden, Marakesh'. We are back in the garden with its distinctive colour pallette. The colours, although still varied are slightly less vivid and the sky is dotted with clouds; this suggests it is Moroccan winter.

We are in a small walled courtyard, the walls are the familiar pale terractoa we see in the Marakesh Medina and the floor is large, glossy vermillion tiles. Reaching over the walls is a spill of branches and foliage, while at their foot are placed large coloured pots at intervals, the palms within them reaching up and casting shifting shadows on the baked plaster behind. In the middle of the space is a small, bubbling fountain: a low white, marble dish, sitting in a blue tiled circle, which in turn sits in a green tiled square, edged with a blue-green mosaic lip of tiles. At each corner of this raised lip is a cobalt blue pot with green foliage emerging from it, forming small leafed domes.

Standing by the fountain are two figures. They are the man and woman from the previous paintings but they are much older than in the first picture. As in the first picture he is wearing a djellaba but this time it is pale green, striped with bronze. The woman wears a floral skirt, dotted with tea roses, and a coral buttoned cardigan. They are holding hands looking down at the fountain. Each has their free hand relaxed at their side and we can see, if we look very carefully at the detail, a wedding band on each. The couples' expressions are serene and accepting.

About Lynne

Lynne Voyce has been widely published in books, magazines and online. She has won and been placed in many short story competitions, including, Momaya, Legend, Flash 500 and Calderdale. Her first solo collection, Kirigami (Ink Tears Press), is currently in pre production and she has completed her first novel. Her work often focuses on the single moment or epiphany, sometimes encorporating magic realism. Her influences are as diverse as the Brontes, Truman Capote, Raymond Carver and Ian Mc Ewan. She is also enjoying the current short story revival.

Before she started writing for publication she wrote for performance, working with theatre groups, live literature promoters and independent film makers. Now she has a family though, she enjoys the solitude of sitting in front of a computer and writing.

A native of Merseyside, after twelve years in Yorkshire, she now teaches in an inner city comprehensive school in Birmingham. She specifically works with students who are considered particularly able in their chosen discipline; this could be academic or practical, as diverse as football and cooking, maths and singing.

In her very precious spare time, she enjoys cinema, reading, travel and comedy. She goes to the gym three times a week, endeavours to cook every night and tries to not drink too much wine.

Paradise for a few hours by Yvonne Walus

What kind of woman hires a sex worker?

The kind who is too lonely in her marriage, yet too preoccupied to have a meaningful affair. The kind who is too shy to pick up a man at a bar.

A woman like me.

Hello and welcome to another day in paradise - perceived. The place is a modern mansion in one of the city's wealthiest suburbs. The time is seven in the morning and the air smells of home-cooked waffles.

"Just coffee for me, thanks." That's Ian, my husband. He's a big shot at an IT firm, and that's all I care to know. There was a time when I could tell you what projects he managed, the names of his clients and colleagues and what development environment they used. Just like there was a time when I had a career and deadlines and a life.

But now Ian is just a big shot in IT. And I'm just a homemaker.

"Just coffee for me too, thanks," mimics my eleven-year old daughter. I'm not that old, honest, it's just that I had children young.

"Eat your breakfast, Mia," I say automatically, then do a mental cringe: exactly when did I turn into my mother?

I light up my third cigarette of the day, careful to exhale through the rancher doors into the garden, as far away as possible from the children.

Ian waves goodbye. We stopped kissing ages ago - I mean the everyday hello and goodbye and you-look-nice kisses. We still do the half-embarrassed tongue-dance when we have sex. When we bother to have sex. If.

Ian blames me. I blame the cancer.

Oh, he is still attentive enough at parties, the perfect ones we throw at our perfect house, or the ones we grace with our presence on other cliff tops. In public, he will stroke my thigh or drop a quick kiss onto my neck when everybody's looking. In private, he avoids bodily contact, as though he imagines the disease infectious.

We are late. I yell Mia and Theo into the car (when the diagnosis came through, I vowed never to yell at my children ever again, and it still makes me feel guilty to slip up). I octopus their belongings into the car. Then I do the school run and the daily work out at the gym.

I know many women envy me my perfectly toned body, my perfect house, my perfect family. That's what I need: I need them to envy me. If they envy me hard enough, who knows, I may even start envying myself.

On the way back home, I stop at a discreet white villa to have sex with a guy at least ten years my junior. He looks gorgeous in his tight black jeans and the shirt he's left unbuttoned.

My hands savour the moment as they slowly explore the bulge of his biceps. I lick my way around his chest and the six-pack on his stomach all the way to the top button on the jeans. Fingers trembling with anticipation, I struggle with the metal stud.

"Here, let me," he murmurs.

I know he won't return the favour. He will French-kiss and fondle and fuck, but he won't go down on his clients. And yet we still pay top dollar for an hour with his body.

When I'm done toying with him, I strip - except for my tube top - and lie face down on the bed. No words: the advantage of being a regular. The only sounds are his quickened breath and the soft Gaelic music permeating the little room.

He selects my favourite oil and caresses it into my shoulders, buttocks and feet. Ten minutes later I turn onto my back and his fingertips print slippery circles into my stomach and thighs. He knows not to stray anywhere near my chest.

Before long, the scent of patchouli does its magic. I open my knees, like a book.

Any bloke would envy me my job. Every morning, I play hide-the-salami, and I get paid to do it, too. It doesn't get much better than that.

My rates dictate that all my clients are rich, and therefore finishing-school polite. They are also rich enough to be well preserved with creams and long days of leisure, with boob lifts and tummy tucks, with Botox or whatever the latest craze. And as it happens, I prefer my women older, anyway.

What I like the most, surprisingly enough, is not the sex. I mean, sex is ultra important when you aren't getting any, but regular sex is overrated. Highly pleasurable, I'll give you that, but still overrated.

No, what I like the most, is the sense of power. My power to give or withhold. My power to fulfil their fantasies.

Every day, I step into my personal bit of paradise, where my body is worshipped with their money. It doesn't matter what they are into: bondage or loving, silk or leather - they all think me their god.

Well, sort of. I don't have a delusion of grandeur. I don't take my role too seriously. Except that I do feel a sense of responsibility towards the women who come to me. They are lonely, they are lost, they are looking for love - and I can't help. All I can do is make them forget their worries. For a few hours, but that's better than nothing, right?

There is this one client, for instance. Cancer. And she hasn't given up the smokes. Kissing her is like licking a cigarette butt. She looks healthy but I know she must be scarred: inside and out. I also know that remission is not forever. My mum was in remission for seven years. We all celebrated at the five-year mark and that's when my mum took up smoking again. In those days, they said that five years was the magic number, but they were wrong. Maybe it was the cigarettes that did it, I don't know. My sister took it hard. Our dad took it even harder: he just disappeared one fine morning, leaving me to look after Bronwyn. So that's what I've been doing. She wants for nothing: the best private school in town, extra lessons, horse riding, school camps. Just like the rich kids.

Anyhow.

Any bloke would envy me. And you know what? They bloody well should. Paradise doesn't come easy and it doesn't come to just anybody.

I'm the lucky one.

Back home, I'm still smiling as I sip my second cup of coffee for the day, light another cigarette and start on the dinner preparations. There is not much more for me to do (ever since I got sick, we've had a cleaner three times a week and the garden services weekly), so I kill time by ironing Ian's business shirts to show him how much I love him.

Kill time.... When the diagnosis came through, time was all I could think about. I wondered how much I had left. I counted every hour I spent with and without the children. I renounced every activity that I disliked, I pruned out every time-filler, I cut out the TV and the chitchat lunches. My life post-diagnosis, the part that wasn't spent on treatment and recovery, was a blueprint for efficiency and time management.

And now? Now I even have time to colour-coordinate the bathroom towels and bake Ian's favourite cake before it's time to taxi my children from school to drama and soccer and homework groups.

This is where my two worlds mesh. The guy from the discreet white villa has a younger sister in the same group as Mia.

When we bumped into each other at the homework group for the first time, it was less awkward than you'd imagine: first was the surprise that usually comes when you see somebody you know in another context, then he extended his hand and introduces himself ("I'm Damian, Bronwyn's brother.") and before I had a chance to react, Mia launched herself into my arms and told me that she was dying for a pair of boots "the very same as Michelle's, Mummy, identical." And that was it.

Today I arrive early, but Damian is already waiting for the children to finish their homework group. Still the same tight jeans that sent electric shivers through me only five hours ago. Still the same shirt, now firmly buttoned up.

"Hi."

"Hi, how are you?" As though we hadn't seen each other earlier this morning.

I reach into my bag for a cigarette.

His hand stops mine. "Should you?"

What I should be is furious with him for mentioning the unmentionable. But instead, all I feel is tired. I shrug off his concern together with his hot fingers. Light up. Inhale.

"Mummy!"

With that one word, I become a different person, a person who doesn't think about men in tight jeans, or patchouli, or cigarettes.

"Let's go get your brother," I hug her tight to what's left of my chest. By the time we're done cuddling, I've forgotten about Damian.

For the rest of the day, I'm a marionette, turning to the strings tugged by my children. Mummy-this, Mummy-that, Mummy-do, Mummy-help, may-I, why-not, I-don't-want-to-eat-carrot, Mummy-come-here-there-is-a big-spider-on-my-bookshelf, another-ten-minutes-Mummy-I -want-to-finish-watching-this.

Ian comes home when the children are already asleep. His eyes are wilted and there are stress lines in his jaw. He eats his dinner in front of the TV, though I will bet my factory-new BMW that he has no idea what he's watching. He gobbles up the cake on autopilot without a thank you.

By the time he switches off the TV, I'm in bed, sheltered by a set of chaste cream silk pyjamas.

He snakes in the bed towards me. "Come on, how about it?"

So much for foreplay.

I turn away. "You know why not."

"I can do you from the back. I won't see a thing."

And so much for sensitivity. I can do you from behind. Whatever happened to You are so beautiful or You look even sexier with your boobs reconstructed or Nipples are way overrated?

"Goodnight, Ian."

"Women," he mutters. Then he raises his voice. "There is just no way to please you, is there? Look around you. You live in paradise. Any half-sane woman would love to trade places with you."

"Yeah," I bite back. "She would have to be only half-sane."

"Bitch!" He switches off his light and turns his face to the wall. The bed vibrates with the regular up-down motion of his fist.

Throat constricted and eyes smarting, I desert the bed and slide out onto the deck. Out of habit, I reach for the cigarettes. I long for the burst of nicotine in my lungs, easing away the tension, ironing out the hurt.

Suddenly I remember the look on Damian's face. His fingers on mine when he tried to stop me.

His fingers on my back massaging away the stress.

His fingers inside me.

I take aim and throw. The white-and-red packet makes a graceful arc through the evening air straight into the pampered clump of flax in the corner. My silver lighter (inscribed "To my darling on our tenth anniversary") follows suit.

And then I climb back into the marital bed, pull the goose down duvet up to my chin, breathe in the faint lemon and lavender scent of my linen that almost masks the odour of Ian's self-indulgence.

So ends another day in the paradise of suburbia. And I know that tomorrow will trace the same pattern in the cosmic makeup of my life. Still, I'm thankful for the hours of today, and I'm thankful that I was given tomorrow to look forward to. Some women without breasts aren't so lucky.

What kind of woman hires a sex worker?

One like me.

One like you.

About Yvonne

Born in Poland, raised in South Africa and currently making New Zealand her home, Yvonne Walus is an internationally published author of murder mysteries and thrillers. Her latest novel, OPERATION: GENOCIDE, published in USA by Stairway Press, is a thriller on one level, but on another it asks important questions about patriotism, relationships and loyalty. Although passionate about her writing, Yvonne believes her two children are her most important creations. When not a mother and wife, she is a slave to two cats and master to one dog.

Links: operationgenocide.com, www.yvonnewalus.com

Little Sisters by Mairi Wilson

The scream sliced into our conversation and I leapt up. Tess rolled her eyes and dragged herself to her feet.

"Here we go again. You wait here. Have more tea."

The scream gave way to sobbing.

"What's going on, you two?" Tess disappeared through the open door to the sitting room, pulling it slightly to behind her. "There's no need for all that noise, Lisa. What kind of a welcome home is this for Auntie Julie?"

"Simon hit me and it hurts!" Lisa wailed.

"I'm sure he didn't mean–"

"Yes he did, Mummy, and he broke my necklace—"

"She was annoying me," Simon's flat voice interrupted his sister's complaint.

"Maybe she was, Simon, but she's younger than you and—"

"Stop picking on me! You always pick on me!" Footsteps thumped out of the room and up the stairs. A door slammed and for a fraction of a second the house was silent.

"Simon!" Tess called after him.

"Mummy, it hurts. My tummy—"

"Shh, Lisa, stop fussing. Simon? Simon!" I heard Tess's slower feet on the stairs and then a knock on a door upstairs.

"Go away. I hate you. You always say it's my fault!"

"Simon, stop shouting, darling. Open the door," his mother placated, their voices floating clearly down the stairs.

"Only if you keep Lisa away. She annoys me!"

"I will, darling, Now open up."

A door opened and closed and then silence. I was stunned. When had all this started? I'd only been away a few months.

There were still faint sobs coming from the sitting room, although they were softer now. I peeped through the crack of the door to the next room. Lisa was hunched on the floor, head down, arms round knees pulled into her chest. As I watched, the sobbing slowed and she sat up, wiping pale cheeks with the back of her hand, and sniffing dramatically. She stood, rubbing her stomach for a moment and then picked up Lolly, her doll, and clutched it to her, nuzzling her cheek against the blonde, synthetic hair.

"There, there, Lolly, don't cry," she crooned. "Mummy'll make it better." Lisa soothed her doll, stroking its round stomach gently, until something on the floor caught her eye. Her face crumpled as she reached for it, still hugging Lolly tightly to her. It was her Princess Pink necklace. And it was broken. As she held it up in front of her, shimmering plastic beads dripped from her hand, bouncing and scattering across the floor.

I went back to the kitchen table and sat down again.

"Lisa? Lisa, can you come and help me with something?"

I heard the creak of floorboards in the hallway.

"Lisa? Are you there?"

Thin fingers curled round the edge of the door and then her face appeared, eyes down and hair flopping forward.

"Lisa, I really need your help."

The head lifted a little so I could see her face as she stepped into the room, clearly intrigued. Lolly had been abandoned and Lisa stood looking at her feet, thumb in mouth. I held my breath and waited.

She gave an exaggerated sigh and then shuffled across the floor to lean sideways against me. I put one arm around her and pulled her close.

"I need you to help me make a card."

One leg hooked over my knew.

"Here, sit up. Look, there's paper here and lots of crayons, but I don't know what to draw."

Still she said nothing. But she settled in my lap, pushing herself upright and taking her thumb out of her mouth. She picked up a purple crayon. I nudged the paper closer to her.

"But I don't know who it's for," she sounded tearful again as she slumped back against me.

"It's for …" I hadn't thought that far ahead. "It's for…umm…"

"Is it for Granny?"

"Yes, of course. Granny."

"Why?"

"Well…it's for Granny because…"

"Is it to say thank you?" She'd sat up and was poking at the other crayons and pencils strewn across the table.

"Yes…Yes, that's it." I had no idea what we were to thank Granny for and hoped she wouldn't ask.

"Granny likes flowers," she sucked thoughtfully on the purple pencil.

"Yes, she does, doesn't she?" We were on safer ground now. The pencil began to move across the page.

"She likes purple and green ones. I gived her some and she put them on the fridge." Lisa dropped purple for green and started to draw big leaves and long stalks. "She can put these ones on the fridge too. What colour for this one?"

"Err…pink? What do you think?"

"Orange."

Soon the page was crammed with leaves and flowers, none of which would shame a granny's fridge and I knew would be given pride of place on my mother's. Lisa was chattering constantly now, describing everything she drew as she drew it, every colour as she picked it, every thought as she thought it; and the hand that had been clutching her stomach was now holding the paper steady whilst she coloured energetically.

By the time I heard a door upstairs, the tears had long gone.

"What's going on here, then?" Tess seemed surprised to find her daughter at the kitchen table.

"We're drawing for Granny," Lisa replied without looking up. "This one's her favourite and she likes this one too." She pointed first to a splash of yellow that might have been a daffodil and then to something blue that I doubted Granny would ever have seen before. Tess rolled her eyes above her daughter's head.

"I hope you're not bothering Auntie Julie, Lisa."

"No, you've been helping me, haven't you, Lisa?" The bent head nodded. "Everything ok?" I asked her mother.

"Yes, more or less. He gets so upset. He can't help it. It's so hard for him."

"Mmm," I said pointedly. "Hard for all of you, I think." I held her gaze and dragged it down with mine to the other child sitting in my lap.

"Oh, she soon gets over it. But he dwells on things, worries about them more. It's his…condition…you know…" I didn't know anything, although I'd wondered. But when I'd once tried to raise the subject, mentioned it was odd the way he recited the dialogue of his favourite DVDs verbatim or insisted on having his books lined up in exactly the right height order, she'd bitten my head off and refused to discuss it.

"Simon's special, Auntie Julie, but I'm not," Lisa voice chipped in to my thoughts.

"Yes you are! Of course you're special." I cuddled her closer to me.

"No, I'm not, am I, Mummy?"

"Well, not in the way that Simon is, no."

"But you're special...in...in other ways..." I couldn't believe this. "Tess? Tell her..."

Her mother laughed. "You'll only confuse her."

There was a crash from upstairs and an angry voice shouted, "Mum! Mum!"

Tess jumped up, looked at me and then with a nervous giggle, sat down again.

"Come here if you want me, Simon, I'm talking to Auntie Julie."

"Mum, come now!"

"Better see what's wrong. He'll only get distressed, otherwise." She disappeared back upstairs.

"I'm not allowed to shout for Mummy but Simon can." I was glad Lisa couldn't see my face.

We drew on in silence, the scratch of crayons the only sound in the kitchen until Tess came back and went straight to the fridge. She poured a glass of milk and got two biscuits out of the tin and went back upstairs without saying a word.

"Hungry," she said, when she finally returned, rolling those eyes again in a way that was beginning to annoy me. "Wouldn't wait for tea. Even though he knows it's early tonight because we walk Lisa round to Little Stars at five and…oh, it's quarter to, already!" Tess's cheeks flushed red. "He won't do anything now till he's finished his milk and…look Lisa, sweetheart, I think you'll have to give it a miss this week. Simon's very upset and he won't want to walk round and you know we can't leave him here on his own, so–"

"I'll take her."

"–I'm sorry but you'll just—"

"Tess. Stop. I'll take her. Lisa, would you like me to take you to Little Stars?" Curls danced madly as she nodded her head. "Right, then. You stay here with Simon, Tess. We'll be fine."

"Oh Julie, would you? Have you got time?"

"Of course I've got time," I bristled.

"I mean, I wouldn't ask but…are you sure you don't mind?"

"You didn't ask, I offered, and of course I don't mind. Come on Lisa, finish that and fetch your coat."

For a second, I thought I saw tears in my little sister's eyes, before she blinked and started tidying up the crayons, tugging the page of flowers out from under Lisa's elbow.

"Do as you're told, Lisa. Don't keep Auntie Julie waiting."

I could hear toys and cushions being thrown to one side and then a few groans and grunts as Lisa struggled with something. She came back in and pirouetted. She was wearing a pair of fairy wings.

Tess groaned. "Not the wings again. She made them in school. They've hardly been off since."

"We painted them and then Miss Maynard sprayed glitter for us." She reached up behind her and fanned the wings. "She said mine were the prettiest."

"They're fab! The best fairy wings I've ever seen. Come on, then. Let's go."

"Wait," Tess said as Lisa skipped across the kitchen, arms flapping. Her mother bent to hug her and kissed the top of her head. "They're the best fairy wings I've ever seen, too, darling." Lisa's smile was beautiful. "Now, off you go," she pushed Lisa towards the door. "I've got to see to Simon."

"Oh yes! Here, Mummy." Lisa took her mother's hand and planted a loud kiss in the middle of its palm. "That's for Simon. I still love him."

Smiling tightly, Tess crossed her arms across her chest, and leant back against the kitchen worktop. I watched in astonishment. Wasn't she going to say anything to this amazing little girl? As I snatched up my car keys, Tess reached out and touched my shoulder.

"Thanks, Julie. It's so good to have my big Sis home. I missed you."

Missed me? All the time I'd been in London, she'd never even called. Not once and…With a pang, I realised I hadn't phoned her either. Not even after Mum said Simon had to go to the educational psychologist, and that Tess refused to talk about it. I'd meant to phone but work was really busy and…and nothing.

I put my hand on hers and squeezed. We stood for a moment watching Lisa stretch up on tiptoes, arms spread, ready to take flight. And then we laughed together as our fairy launched herself off the step and danced down the path towards the car flapping shimmering wings as she went, a sparkling reminder of just how precious sisters can be.

About Mairi

Mairi currently divides her time between Scotland and Spain. Her work has appeared online, on radio, in a number of journals and publications including *Gutter*, *The Eildon Tree* and *Pushing out the Boat*, and in performance at Edinburgh and other festivals. To date she's written mostly poetry, but has more recently had a number of short stories published, and is nearly finished with a novel set, not surprisingly, in Scotland and Spain.

When she's not writing she teaches English as a foreign language, occasionally reverts to a former life as a marketing consultant, or develops and runs workshops on creative writing, communications, presentation skills or anything else involving words and fiction.

About The Hysterectomy Association

The Hysterectomy Association provides impartial, timely and appropriate information and support to women. It was founded in the mid 1990's by Linda Parkinson-Hardman who is the author of several books about hysterectomy, online business and one novel.

It is based in Dorset in the UK and you can find out more about the association through the following accounts:

Website: hysterectomy-association.org.uk

Facebook: facebook.com/HysterectomyUK

Twitter: twitter.com/HysterectomyUK

LinkedIn: linkedin.com/company/the-hysterectomy-association

Other books from The Hysterectomy Association include:

- 101 Handy Hints for a Happy Hysterectomy

- In My Own Words: Women's Experience of Hysterectomy

- Losing the Woman Within

- The Pocket Guide to Hysterectomy

- A Diva's Guide to the Menopause - Short Story

- Hysteria Anthologies

You can connect directly with Linda on her blog at www.womanontheedgeofreality.com.

www.ingramcontent.com/pod-product-compliance
Lightning Source LLC
Chambersburg PA
CBHW021135130626
46554CB00002B/975